SECOND SUMMER WITH LADIS

ACORN LIBRARY

LUCY BOSTON *The Castle of Yew*
HELEN CLARE *Seven White Pebbles*
EILEEN COLWELL *A Hallowe'en Acorn*
GRISELDA GIFFORD *Ben's Expedition*
The Mystery of the Wooden Legs
KENNETH GRAHAME *The Reluctant Dragon*
RENÉ GUILLOT *Nicolette and the Mill*
Pascal and the Lioness
Rex and Mistigri
Tipiti the Robin
MARGARET HAINSON *A Christmas Acorn*
ANITA HEWETT *Piccolo*
Piccolo and Maria
KATHLEEN HUNT *A Midsummer Acorn*
WILLIAM MACKELLAR *Davie's Wee Dog*
BETTY ROLAND *The Forbidden Bridge*
Jamie's Discovery
Jamie's Summer Visitor
JOSÉ MARIA SANCHEZ-SILVA *The Boy and the Whale*
Ladis and the Ant
Second Summer with Ladis
DAVID STEPHEN *Rory the Roebuck*
FRANK R. STOCKTON *The Griffin and the Minor Canon*
with CHARLES DICKENS *The Magic Fishbone*
CATHERINE STORR *Lucy*
Lucy Runs Away
PAMELA SYKES *Billy's Monster*

Second Summer with Ladis

JOSÉ MARIA SANCHEZ-SILVA

Translated from the Spanish by Isabel Quigly

Illustrated by
DAVID KNIGHT

ACORN LIBRARY

THE BODLEY HEAD
LONDON SYDNEY
TORONTO

El Segundo Verano de Ladis
(Editorial Marfil, S. A., 1968)

Second Summer with Ladis
(London, The Bodley Head, 1969)

SBN 370 00906 1
© José Maria Sanchez-Silva 1967
English translation © The Bodley Head Ltd 1969
Illustrations © The Bodley Head Ltd 1969
Printed and bound in Great Britain for
The Bodley Head Ltd
9 Bow Street, London WC2
by William Clowes and Sons Ltd, Beccles
Set in Monotype Plantin
First published by Editorial Marfil, S. A. 1967
First published in Great Britain 1969

Chapter I

All through the year Ladis was waiting for the summer holidays.

'How much longer?' he asked his mother in the spring.

'Only four months,' she said, as if four months were half-an-hour.

'Four months,' sighed Ladis. 'That's practically another year.'

Spring had come early. Out in the damp, dirty yard of the house in Madrid where Ladis lived, he noticed a few insects, pale, small creatures and terribly quick. Tiny flies were already about as well. Ladis picked them up and studied them. He realized that he needed to see them rather better.

'Could I have a magnifying glass?' he asked his father that night at supper.

His father looked thunderstruck.

'A magnifying glass?'

'So that I can see small creatures better,' said Ladis.

'Is it so important?'

To Ladis it was important. For Ladis had a secret. During the previous summer holidays on his uncle's farm in the country, he had made friends with an ant. He had talked to her a great deal and had even got inside the ants' nest, and had flown higher than the dragonflies and the grasshoppers. Mufra, his ant friend, was the Queen of her nest, and could make him as small as a glow-worm whenever he wanted. He was longing for the time when he could visit her again. And yet he couldn't talk about it! He realised that if he did, people would just laugh. Everyone would think it an enormous lie. He could not tell his father why he was so interested in studying insects.

'A magnifying glass would cost a fortune,' his father said.

Ladis had a good idea.

'Well, it would cost the same as glasses, and as I don't need to wear glasses . . .'

He got his magnifying glass. It was a clumsy one and secondhand, with a black metal handle, but to Ladis it seemed perfect and he took it to school to show his friends. It didn't magnify things much because really good magnifying glasses are small ones, but Ladis's eyes were extremely good so he didn't need much help.

No one at school had a great deal of time to use the magnifying glass. This was because the teacher had asked all the nine-year-olds to make a special effort in their exams. Ladis tried to get good marks, for he knew it was very hard for his father to keep him at school. Some boys he knew couldn't go at all. But the main reason for working hard was that his father had told him that if he did not he wouldn't go to the farm that summer.

As a result he came third in his class. He had

such good marks and was so keen on insects that his teacher lent him a picture book on natural history and a small book on ants, which were his favourites.

'Read them, draw the animals you like best in your exercise book, and give it back to me when you come back after the holidays,' she told him.

That evening, Ladis packed his suitcase. The two books lay open on a chair, but he wasn't going to read them yet. He wanted to save that up for the farm and make them last for ages.

'Ladis, supper!' called his mother.

Ladis put the magnifying glass at the bottom of his suitcase, and then shut the two books and put them very carefully under his pillow. His teacher had put a bright green plastic cover on each of them to prevent it getting dirty.

He switched off the light and went to have supper.

The best part of the year was coming now.

Chapter II

Ladis travelled to the farm alone. After going there the previous summer he knew the journey. This year he went by bus to the nearby town, where the van driver met him. At the farm gate his uncle and aunt were waiting for him, with Trickster, the dog. There were hugs and kisses all round while the van driver drove up to the house to leave Ladis's suitcase and the packet of presents he had brought.

Uncle Floro and Aunt Lola were exactly the same as they had been last year, but Ladis, it seemed, was not.

'You *have* grown a lot,' said Aunt Lola.

The van came back. 'Thank you, Quique,' said Uncle Floro.

'A pleasure,' said Quique, slowing down; and then, to Ladis: 'Have a good time, lad! I'll come and fetch you, like last year.'

The van set off and Ladis ran on ahead to the farm; he was dying to see his other old friends and, with Trickster tagging along, went straight to the stable, scaring the hens who whirled stupidly about the middle of the yard. The stable looked strangely empty. Noble, the cart-horse, stared at Ladis gravely and kindly, but clearly didn't remember him.

'Where is the donkey?' asked Ladis, in dismay.

'He died, Ladis,' said Uncle Floro, sadly. 'He was ill and the vet said he had pneumonia and we must give him lots of medicine. But it wasn't any good. One morning when I went into the stable I found him dead. Noble who was tied up beside him was so upset that he kicked me, which he's never done before.'

There were tears in Ladis's eyes as he looked at the gentle horse. He said nothing but hurried out into the cowshed so that his uncle should not see he was crying. Immediately his sadness was forgotten. Beside Patch, the cow, was a white calf with a very sweet face. Ladis stared in delight, while Uncle Floro and Aunt Lola smiled at him from the door.

'He hasn't got a name yet,' said Aunt Lola. 'We wanted you to name him when you came.'

'There isn't a single mark on him!' said Ladis.

'That's true,' said Uncle Floro, surprised.

'Then I've thought of a name for him,' said Ladis.

'What's that?' asked Aunt Lola.

'Spotless,' said Ladis, laughing. 'He's the son of Patch and he's got no marks. So we'll call him Spotless.'

Uncle Floro and Aunt Lola laughed too, and Ladis hugged Spotless, gazing into his great wet, friendly eyes. Patch didn't seem too pleased with all this affection: maybe she was jealous.

They went into Uncle Floro's small house.

On the way Ladis remembered his tame sparrow, Piccolo. But Aunt Lola said they had seen nothing more of him.

'When you set him free from his cage he must have found it too hard to survive.'

Indoors his uncle and aunt had another surprise in store for Ladis. He discovered Sooty, the cat, in a straw basket, and beside him were two restless black kittens.

'Are they his children?' asked Ladis.

'They are,' said Aunt Lola.

'But where's the mother?' asked Ladis, looking round.

'Sooty is a female,' said Uncle Floro laughing.

'Then we shall have to call her Mrs Sooty,' said Ladis, picking up the two kittens while Mrs Sooty watched him, ready to leap on him if he did anything to hurt them.

Ladis had now seen all his old friends except the most important of all, Mufra the ant. Ever since he had arrived at the farm he had been looking at the ground and gazing about him, searching for her. But she couldn't yet have known he had come. It was nearly supper-time and there was no time for anything else. Ladis took out the presents, which delighted Uncle Floro and Aunt Lola. He had brought his uncle some tobacco and a safety razor, and his aunt a bottle of eau de Cologne and some stockings, which she examined happily in the light of the lamp.

'These are too fine for me,' she said.

All the excitement had given Ladis an appetite and he ate a good supper. But he soon felt sleepy. When he said goodnight he asked: 'Can I go out as soon as I wake up tomorrow?'

'Of course,' said Uncle Floro. 'But what's the hurry?'

'It's just that I want to see everything right away.'

'Do be careful down at the lake, won't you?'
Aunt Lola began.

But Ladis was already dropping with sleep,
and so she took him off to bed.

Chapter III

Next morning, when Ladis awoke, Uncle Floro and Aunt Lola were already up. He had not yet got used to country ways. The sun had not woken him, as he had thought it would. So, before he could get outside, he had to drink a big glass of bread-and-milk. He was already far away when he heard Aunt Lola's voice calling:

'Mind the lake!'

Ladis laughed. He wasn't going anywhere near it. He ran to the tree he had marked with his knife, beyond which was Mufra's ant nest. How often he had thought of her!

Panting with eagerness, Ladis reached the tree he thought was the right one, but couldn't be sure if it was. Wind and rain, caterpillars and springtime, had all changed its shape. Last summer Ladis had put some tiles over the nest to protect it from the rain. But he could not find them either. Uncle Floro must have taken them away. Feeling terribly disappointed, he went gloomily back to the house.

'Did you take some tiles away, down there?' he asked Uncle Floro.

'Was it you who put them there?'

'I put them there to cover an ants' nest.'

'Well, I picked them up ages ago, but I don't remember seeing an ants' nest.'

And Uncle Floro carried on with his work.

Ants, Ladis reflected, were really very clever; whenever there was any danger, or simply when they thought it was going to rain or get colder, they shut the openings of their nests. He spent the rest of the morning with his new friend, Spotless, who kept rushing at him and butting him with his big head in a friendly, funny way. Later he took the kittens out into the sun and watched them lapping up a plateful of milk.

In the afternoon he worked with Uncle

Floro. Ladis didn't find Mufra, though. He found several ants' nests as he went about the farm, but the ants in them were different. Uncle Floro was pleased with Ladis's new interest, especially when he used his magnifying glass and called him to look at one of the insects.

But without Mufra, Ladis thought, the summer would be ruined. He began to feel melancholy, and unpacked the books his teacher had lent him. Uncle Floro and Aunt Lola protested.

'You have come to get fresh air and sunshine, to bathe and run about and take exercise,' they said. 'Books are for when you're in town.'

Suddenly Ladis had an idea.

'Where did you bury the poor donkey, Uncle Floro?' he asked.

'Near the lake. But don't you go there—I didn't bury him very deep and he may have gone bad.'

But Ladis went along. He took Trickster with him, which was a great help because he found the scent. Near the lake, Ladis saw long lines of ants and several beetles. A large water rat slipped away. Ladis felt sorry and slightly sick, for he knew the creatures must be using the donkey's body for food. He couldn't see or smell anything, though. The insects must have made underground tunnels.

The next day Uncle Floro and Aunt Lola took Ladis for an outing to the seaside. He had never seen the sea and when he looked at it he said nothing. He spent a happy day and bathed among the rocks with Uncle Floro, while Aunt Lola paddled. Ladis thought the sea was too big. He remembered Mufra. That is, he never stopped remembering her and when he thought of her, so small and clever, so good, so important, while he was looking at the enormous sea, he felt he loved her more than ever.

That night, Ladis wrote about the sea in his

diary. On the bedside table stood a thin candle that gave a very clear light. The shadows shifted in the breeze that came through the window. Far away, he heard a cricket. Occasionally an owl hooted gloomily. But between the sounds, like a great precipice suddenly opening up between mountains, the silence returned.

'Ladis,' said a small voice beside him.

Ladis raised his pencil from the exercise book and listened. Nothing. But he thought . . .

'Ladis,' said the small voice, again.

There was no doubt about it now. Ladis looked at the pillow, in the bed, along the wall. At last, on the bedside table beside the candle, he saw Mufra and picked her up in his hand.

'You're stifling me,' she said.

Ladis sat down on the bed again and opened his hand under the light. Shinier than ever, Mufra was tidying herself up after the slight upheaval she had suffered in Ladis's hand.

'I've been looking for you the whole time,' said Ladis.

'It was only today that I heard you had arrived,' said Mufra. 'If you hadn't been to where the donkey is buried I wouldn't have known it yet.'

'Have you left the nest?'

'We couldn't help it.'

'What happened?'

'It will take a long time to tell you. Are you sleepy?'

'No.'

But Mufra knew he was.

'I saw the sea.'

'What was it like?'

'Very big . . . I thought about you.'

'Because I'm very small, you mean?'

'I don't know. But all the time I kept remembering you. Was it a very bad winter?'

'That's something we don't know ourselves, quite often.'

'What do you mean?'

'Well, during the winter we look for the deepest places in the nest, so as to get away from the cold, and we hibernate most of the time.'

'What does hibernate mean?'

'It means being asleep, more or less, not eating or drinking, lying quite still in a corner with your legs folded up to your body.'

'Oh!'

Ladis was very happy to have found his dear Mufra again, but very tired as well, because he had been to the sea that day. His eyes were nearly shut.

'You must undress and get into bed,' said Mufra.

'But you are here.'

'That doesn't matter. I'm going to stay with you a long time and tell you everything that's happened, but before that you must get into bed. Hurry up, blow out the candle.'

24

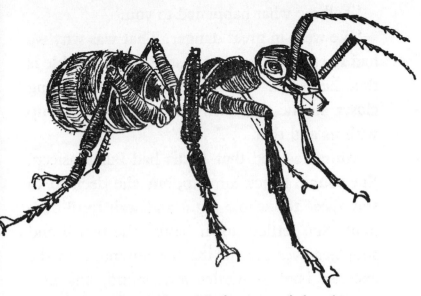

Ladis realised that Mufra was right; he put her on the bedside table, blew out the candle and undressed. In a moment he was in bed with the sheet over him.

'Mufra,' he said, softly, 'are you there?'

'Yes,' said the small voice.

'Can you see me?'

'Of course I can. I'm sitting on your exercise book, beside the pencil.'

'Tell me what happened to you.'

'We were in great danger. That was why we had to escape from our nest. But the trouble is that the danger has followed us, and it's getting closer all the time. Any day it may catch up with us and then . . .'

Mufra realised that Ladis had fallen asleep. She couldn't tuck him up, but she decided to stay there the whole night and wait until daylight. She settled down beside the pencil and shut her eyes too, laying her antennae on the exercise book to notice any sound, any new smell, any danger.

Chapter IV

It was the longest night of Mufra's life, because in the fine warm weather she needed very little sleep to feel rested. She looked at Ladis, noticed how regularly he was breathing, and went for a walk round the pencil; then she went off to sleep again, and woke up again ten minutes later. At this point she decided to go out and look for some of her fast dragonflies who were the ants' 'aeroplanes'. When she returned, there was a glow in the eastern sky, and she decided to wake Ladis.

It wasn't easy. Compared with Mufra, Ladis was a mountain. Any careless movement he made might squash her. She began at his feet, which were now uncovered, and tried to tickle him between the toes. But nothing happened. She walked slowly up to one of his knees. Still nothing happened. Then she spent a while on his chest, terrified of his heavy heartbeats that sounded like some great engine pumping.

Very bravely she climbed over to his left ear and began to tickle it, hard. Before Ladis's hand had reached it, Mufra had leapt on to the pillow and was screeching at the top of her voice:

'Ladis!'

Ladis awoke. The sun had very nearly risen and the room was lightening. Suddenly he remembered what had happened.

'Mufra, did you call me?' he said.

'I don't know how often I've called you!'

Ladis sat up in bed.

'Have I been asleep for long?'

'Seven hours on end.'

Ladis picked Mufra up in his hand and then suddenly started.

'What are you doing?' said Mufra, terrified.

'It's my magnifying glass,' answered Ladis, reassuringly.

It seemed absurd that he hadn't yet thought of looking at Mufra through the magnifying glass. He did so, and for the first time saw three small rings in a triangle on her head, close to the white spots that had so often allowed him to recognise her.

'What are those little holes?'

'Those are my front eyes,' she said.

'So you've got five eyes?'

'They're not much use to me. We can see only for a very short distance, as you know, and much better with the side eyes than with the others. But do leave that thing alone and be serious.'

Mufra sounded so grave that Ladis put down the magnifying glass.

'Now listen carefully, Ladis. When you fell asleep last night I was telling you that we ran into very great danger. A race of ants that wants to drive us away has appeared in this part of the country. They are smaller than us but fiercer. They're known as Argentine ants all over the world. They're very important because there are so many of them: imagine, in a single summer a community can increase from a hundred to ten thousand!'

'Can't you fight them?'

'Of course we can, but we've got a lot of disadvantages. They are very quick, brave, greedy ants, and very intelligent as well. They can even kill birds and chicks and eat them.'

'And can't anything be done about them?'

'Oh yes, of course,' said Mufra. 'Men invent poisons to fight them, because they get into houses and eat things, but . . .'

'Well, how did they get here?' said Ladis.

'It's quite simple: they came, first of all, in the van that took you away last summer, and came back with a cargo of grain for fodder. Much later the ants' explorers managed to get to where the donkey is buried and found our nest. We had to flee with anything we could carry—children, food, everything.'

'If you tell me where they are, couldn't I destroy their nest?' said Ladis.

Mufra was furious.

'Ladis! I'm not asking you to do anything like that.'

'But you say they are bad, you say they attack people and that people kill them. So why can't I?'

'They're ants, Ladis, you must understand.'

'Well, I shall do it anyway.'

Mufra became really angry and her tone of voice changed.

'Then you'll never see me again,' she said. 'Promise me you won't harm them.'

Ladis promised.

'But why?' he asked.

'Because in things like this you have got to obey me. I'm older than you.'

Ladis burst out laughing.

'Older than me? Why, I'm nearly ten!'

'And I'm twelve,' said Mufra.

'As old as that?' said Ladis, surprised.

'Sometimes we live to be fifteen,' said the ant. 'But look, we're wasting time. Get dressed and we'll be off. I must show you our new nest, where I'm keeping a little memento for you.'

'A memento?'

'Yes, but get dressed. Then you'll see.'

When Ladis was dressed Mufra pricked his foot and he became smaller and smaller, protesting as he did so:

'Not here, not here, Uncle Floro might come in.'

'He won't. They are both asleep and when they get up they will think you're asleep as well. A couple of hours will do for us, and then you can come back.'

When Ladis was the same size as Mufra, she took him on her back and began to climb off the bed. How huge it looked now! The pencil was like a great log, the exercise book like a football field. Mufra ran across the floor with Ladis and started climbing up the wall towards the window.

'We can't go through the window. It's got wire netting on it, to keep insects out.'

'You tuck down your head, and see what a

lot of good that wire netting is!' said Mufra,
without pausing.

And she got through one of the holes quite
easily and climbed down with her cargo on to the

sill, where a dragonfly was waiting for them.

'Good morning,' said Ladis.

'She doesn't know any languages,' said Mufra.

They climbed up on to the beautiful creature's back and it flew off. Not a word was said
on the journey because the wind whistled past,
making breathing difficult, and talking im-
possible. When they reached the end of the trip
and Ladis and Mufra had dismounted, Ladis
couldn't recognise the place. They were on a
low mound where the trees grew in a few
scattered clumps.

'We're very near the lake,' said Mufra.

The ants guarding the land near the nest
approached Mufra respectfully and exchanged
impressions with her, through their antennae.
Some of the older ants recognised Ladis, and
rubbed up against him in a friendly way. But
Ladis wanted to see the surprise Mufra was
keeping for him, and they went into the nest.

They walked along unlit passages and halls,
narrow alleyways and wide corridors crammed
with ants.

'In spite of our losses on the flight,' said

Mufra, 'we are much more crowded here.'

Ladis noticed everything, and realised that a great many things had changed since last year. It was hotter, it smelt more like a chemist's shop, the ventilation was not so good and it was much more untidy, at least on the face of it. He saw a number of parasites and visitors who were not ants. The only ones he could name were greenflies.

Suddenly Mufra stopped him and began burrowing in a pile of earth. Gradually a long object that seemed covered in hairs appeared, and finally Mufra put this object into Ladis's arms.

'What's this?' said Ladis.

'Look at it carefully.'

'It looks like a feather.'

'It is a feather. It's a feather from your bird, Piccolo.'

'So he did die?'

'Yes,' said Mufra. 'The black beetles buried

him, but we got there in time to share the feast.'

'You ate him, then?'

'He was already dead,' said Mufra apologetically. 'And you people eat birds yourselves.'

'Well anyway,' said Ladis, 'thank you very much for this memento. Poor old Piccolo!'

'Maybe if you hadn't set him free he would still be alive.'

'That's what Aunt Lola says.'

'Ah, you see, we're both women,' said Mufra seriously, leading Ladis away.

'Couldn't I see him?' Ladis asked when they were outside.

'You would just see a mound of little bones and you'd be so sad.'

Ladis was silent and sat down on the floor. Mufra, beside him, went back to the subject that was tormenting her.

'Well, as you see, we're here only temporarily. We've had a few isolated skirmishes between our fighters and the vanguard of the Argentine ants. They may attack us when we least expect it and then we shall be done for.'

'I could take you to the other side of the lake in Uncle Floro's boat,' said Ladis.

'That wouldn't make any difference. The new ants are all over the farm. They are on the other side of the lake as well.'

'Do you know what they remind me of?' said Ladis, suddenly remembering the history he knew. 'They remind me of the Greeks and the Romans, when they conquered the whole world, one country after another . . .'

There was a long silence. An ant came up to Mufra with a message. Mufra dismissed her and said:

'The dragonfly is on its way. We must go back. We've spent more than two hours here.'

When the dragonfly appeared Mufra told Ladis:

'We've made a treaty with the dragonflies. We're trying to build up our strength to withstand the Argentine attack when it comes.'

They climbed on to the dragonfly, and soon they were back at Ladis's house and said goodbye.

'Now, can you find us on your own?' Mufra asked.

'Yes,' said Ladis. 'And look—next time we meet will you tell me your life story?'

'Yes, I'll tell you,' said Mufra.

'And will you let me know if you are in danger?'

'I'll think about it.'

And while Ladis breathed deeply to make him return to his normal size, the dragonfly, with Mufra on its back, vanished into the air.

Chapter V

All day, and until he slept that night, Ladis was thinking of the danger from the Argentine ants. Mufra's 'I'll think about it' had left him uneasy. Suppose they turned up in their millions and killed everyone, without his being able to do a thing? But he had promised not to, anyway!

Next day, as he turned it over in his mind, Ladis found an almost perfect solution: he couldn't intervene himself, but Uncle Floro hadn't made any promises. Armed with his magnifying glass, Ladis began searching for the enemy near the house. It was very difficult, but in the end he found not only two nests which he recognised as belonging to the Argentine ants but a small trickle of them going into the stable where Patch and Spotless were. Ladis was delighted and waited until after the

siesta he was made to take—which was the worst part of the day for him, because he was never sleepy after dinner.

Later in the afternoon he followed the trail from the stable to a hole in the yard, and then to Aunt Lola's pantry. Here was a splendid reason for action! He rushed off to Uncle Floro and asked him to come, and then showed him the nests, and the rows of ants going through the stable, the yard and the pantry, endlessly returning, loaded up.

'Why, the rascals! So that's why I sometimes find them even in the bread!'

But he really had no idea what to do.

Ladis told him about what it said in his book: DDT powder. But Uncle Floro saw the danger at once.

'But what about Trickster and the cats?' he said. 'Wouldn't they be poisoned?'

'They don't like the same things as ants,' said Ladis. 'And besides, if you kept them

away for a few days . . .'

Uncle Floro was persuaded. Next day they would go into town. Ladis was delighted. He

hadn't taken the decision himself: Uncle Floro
had. And anyway, Mufra would never know.

The Argentines would be killed and Mufra's ants would be safe. Apart from using DDT, Uncle Floro was going to stop up the nests and cover the holes they had bored inside the house with cement, to cut their lines of communication.

Next day, what with going into town and back in the cart, and buying the DDT and a few other things Aunt Lola needed, they had no time for anything else; but on the following day they completed 'Operation Poison', as Ladis called it. He was pleased and decided to go along and see Mufra, feeling sure that the life story she was going to tell him would be very exciting.

'But it isn't really,' she said, when he saw her a few hours later. 'And before telling it, I want to tell you that this business which is worrying us is getting worse. Something must have happened to our enemies in the nests near your house, because our spies have seen them

46

coming this way in their thousands, so it's very much worse than it was.'

Mufra did not notice Ladis give a start. He realised that this might be because of the poison. He had done exactly the opposite of what he hoped to do! Instead of killing the enemy, he had simply driven them from their homes and made them fiercer than ever. But he said nothing about all this to Mufra.

'Are you quite sure you couldn't hold out against them if they attacked?' he said.

'Well, of course we would do something! We would defend our food, our children and our homes to the end, but . . .'

Mufra's voice had become melancholy and Ladis tried to distract her.

'Well, don't go making excuses for not telling me your life story.'

'Oh, of course, my life story,' said Mufra, settling herself comfortably. 'Well, I've travelled a lot, Ladis, I know a great deal of the world.'

'But are you Spanish?'

'Of course I am. And proud of it. My first trip abroad was to England, in a cargo of raisins from Alicante. I spent some time there and founded a pretty important colony. Then I crossed the Channel to France, in a boat carrying machinery. I stayed there for a while as well and then travelled with a cargo of fruit tree seeds to South America, where I founded more nests. There I met some Argentine ants and learnt a great many things, such as the art of stitching leaves and growing a kind of mushroom we're very fond of.'

'And have you been to Africa?'

'Yes, I have, indeed I have. I came back from South America in some wheat and there I was captured by an entomologist.'

'What's that?'

'A man who studies insects. I lived with some of my sisters in a glass jar full of earth and covered over, so that we would work in

48

the dark, the way we like it, and he could watch us whenever he wanted to. Once I was held by this man's tweezers very close to his magnifying glass. He had a single huge eye. But I realised he didn't want to hurt us and I waited for a chance to escape. I've been in lots of frightful wars, Ladis, I've had thousands of children, I've been a slave in South America...'

Ladis was gazing admiringly at Mufra.

'How you've been around!' he said. 'That's why you know so much and especially why you can talk.'

Mufra gazed silently ahead.

'All this is ending, Ladis,' she said at last.

'Listen,' said Ladis, delighted with a new idea. 'Here on this farm, are there lots of ants' nests of your own kind, founded by you or your children?'

'Ten or twelve.'

'Then why don't we warn them about the trouble you are having so that they can prepare to help against the Argentine ants?'

'It's a good idea,' said Mufra 'but they will have enough to do defending themselves.'

Ladis understood, and was silent for a moment. Then:

'You must hate these ants a lot,' he said. 'Don't you?'

'No,' said Mufra, surprised. 'You mustn't hate anyone. I'll talk to you about that some day. Now you must go home. One of our dragonflies will take you, if you like.'

'No, thanks,' said Ladis, standing up. He took a deep breath and began to return to his normal size. 'I'd sooner learn the way myself, because I had a bit of trouble finding you.'

He picked Mufra up and said:

'Please be sure and tell me when your hour of danger comes.'

He spoke so vehemently and so lovingly that Mufra gave way. 'If a dragonfly lands on your hair, that will be the signal,' she said.

50

Ladis kissed her and let her go near the nest, then started back for home. He was carrying his magnifying glass and stopped to see for himself where the Argentine ants really were. For the first time that summer, he got in late for a meal.

'Wherever have you been?' said Aunt Lola.

'I've been looking for those ants.'

'But I've been calling you all over the place,' said Uncle Floro.

They sat down to their meal and Ladis told them what he had discovered.

'There are millions of them,' he said, with his mouth full.

He thought that if he could only get his Uncle interested they might cut the Argentine ants' route to the lake, that is, to Mufra's nest.

'They don't stop in their nests,' he went on. 'They get about much faster than ordinary ants. You can see they're much busier and that they're getting ready for something really important. My book says that wherever they go they get rid of all the other ants.'

'That's something we could do with,' said Uncle Floro, laughing. 'We could let them get rid of the others and then kill them off as well. That way we'd clean up the whole farm.'

But Ladis disliked this idea and changed the subject.

'There are quite a lot of the ones we call "mad ants" at school, as well. They're the ones who keep dashing around and never get anywhere. It looks as if they live alone and don't have any nests. There are pictures of them in my book and when they're excited or in danger they do something very odd: they can stand on their hind legs, to shoot their poison out better.'

'Eat up and don't talk so much,' said Aunt Lola. 'There's no stopping you.'

Just at that moment, they heard the first thunderclap of the summer.

'Storms already,' said Uncle Floro. 'That's because the spring was so warm.'

'Is the summer over?' said Ladis, terribly worried.

'No, old chap,' said Uncle Floro soothingly. 'But we'll be getting lots of storms and sultry weather.'

It rained the whole afternoon.

Chapter VI

Next day, when Ladis was very quietly trying to make Sooty let Trickster play with her kittens, a dragonfly perched on his head. At first Ladis remembered nothing and flicked it away with his hand, but it came back to land on his head and tickle him through his hair. Then Ladis remembered and dashed out, already feeling hopeless. The Argentine ants' attack—that was it!

He ran as he had never run before, but remembered to stamp on the enemy's nests whenever he found them. Suppose Mufra saw him! When he arrived at the nest he found everything quiet, and, astonished, he sat down on the ground. An ant was coming slowly towards him and Ladis recognised her and began taking off his shoes. Then she pricked his toe and he began getting smaller.

'You tricked me!' said Ladis.

Mufra burst out laughing.

'I wanted to see how long you would take, don't you see? What's the use of warning you of danger unless I know how long it will take you to get here?'

Ladis understood and, still panting, said:

'Well, I suppose you're right, but you had me fearfully worried.'

'I've got something new for you to see,' said Mufra. 'That's why I sent for you—that's the only reason. But don't worry: when the attack really comes I won't send you a dragonfly, I'll come for you myself, on a grasshopper. And now, look at the nest.'

Ladis looked and saw nothing new. It was late afternoon, and the ground was still damp from the previous day's storm. The sun was setting behind the pine trees, in the west. It was a splendid evening, with a bright blue sky and the air very clear after the recent rain; all the colours looked newly painted. Then, from the nest, Ladis saw the large warrior ants coming out and forming two long lines, as if protecting someone very important who would soon be coming out of the nest. Small winged ants then began to come out.

'What's happening?' said Ladis, surprised.

'Those are the new female ants, who are going to mate today,' said Mufra.

'Winged ants?' said Ladis.

'We all have wings at some time in our lives,' Mufra said.

'Have the males got them as well?'

'Yes, they have too, but the males . . .' Here she stopped and went on more seriously, 'In nature, you see, the males are less important than the females. They don't live long and their only function is to fertilize us. But look, look! Don't miss it!'

The new ants looked very fine in their bridal clothes. Their wings shone like silk in the sun-

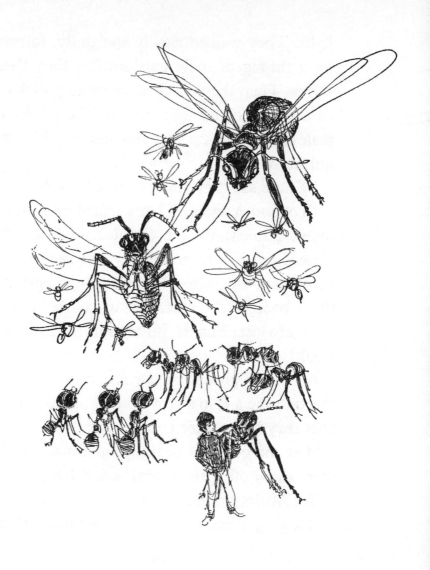

light. They walked slowly and dully, followed by a throng of male ants smaller than themselves. Then they climbed up on to a stick or a stone and took off into the air, followed by the males; they flew up very fast and very high and quickly vanished.

'Where are they going?' asked Ladis.

'To find a mate. That's called the nuptial flight. Afterwards the females, who are fertilized, fall to the ground, where the workers pick them up, bite off their wings and take them back to the nest. But of course most of them are lost. That is, if they survive that long! Look!'

A small group of swifts was swooping through the air, in sharp-beaked pursuit of the ants they knew were now mating.

'Let me get back to my proper size and I'll scare them off with stones!' cried Ladis.

But Mufra grabbed him.

'Don't get excited, Ladis,' she said. 'It's always been this way.' A few couples returned from their flight and came down to earth, clinging together.

'Now, those that don't get back to the nest start the most difficult and most wonderful part of their lives, as I did when I was young.'

'What do they do?'

'Well, each ant seeks a shelter and lives alone, until she lays her eggs. When they hatch and the children grow, she feeds them and they form a family and later a new nest. But until then the ant suffers from hunger and thirst, and lives alone, in every sort of danger, without anyone to help her.'

'But I thought ants only mated in the spring.'

'No,' said Mufra, 'it happens when there are new ants and the earth is softened by rain and the nests can be dug. I've seen matings in every season of the year.'

'And what about Argentine ants—do they

mate in the air as well?'

'No, they don't.'

Suddenly, a terrifying thing happened: a great greenish brown crocodile appeared in front of Mufra, open-jawed, and Ladis, although terribly frightened, dashed between the two of them. The dragon was armed with very sharp teeth and had fierce nails on each of its four legs, and was settling back on its long tail before pouncing on its victim.

'Breath deeply, Ladis,' screamed Mufra.

Ladis understood: this terrible crocodile was an ordinary lizard, but while he was tiny it had the power of a real crocodile. He thought for a moment, and felt ashamed of going back to his proper size without having struck a single blow. The lizard was staring at him, slightly surprised, as it had never seen a man as small as Ladis, and had quite forgotten Mufra. It must have been thinking that, if this little creature was human, he would fit into its mouth just as

well as two or three ants, and it made ready to grab him.

Ladis seized a stick as a weapon, and when the crocodile jumped he jammed it inside its mouth, as he had read of people doing in India. In spite of this Ladis was trapped under the body of the terrible dragon, which was covered in horny scales. Mufra leaped on to the lizard and jabbed at its eyes; the creature retreated, but made ready to come straight back and attack again.

'Breathe deeply, or it will kill us,' yelled Mufra.

Ladis obeyed. At the first breath he took he started growing, while the lizard gazed at him, fascinated.

'Harder, Ladis, breathe harder,' cried Mufra.

When Ladis was about eighteen inches tall the lizard bolted in terror. Here was a tale to tell its grandchildren, when it had some!

They were free of the monster at last, and Ladis, who had been terribly scared, began giggling nervously.

'You're awfully brave,' said Mufra.

'Well, only because you were in front of me,' said Ladis nobly. 'If I had been alone he would have gobbled me up.'

Both of them laughed. For a while they

stayed and watched the ant couples returning.
Suddenly Ladis thought of something.

'Mufra,' he said. 'Who was it killed Piccolo?'

'The same chap who killed the donkey:
winter.'

'I'd like to put a white stone where he was
buried, so that he would always be remembered.'

'And so you shall. Next time we meet I'll
take you to where poor Piccolo is buried.'

Mufra then arranged for a dragonfly to take
Ladis quickly home.

'Drink a little wine when you get back!'

'Why?' said Ladis, already astride the dragonfly.

'Because you've had a fright,' said Mufra
laughing.

And the dragonfly set off.

Chapter VII

For a few days the weather was dull and rainy. Ladis took the chance of doing some reading and discovering more about ants from the books his teacher had lent him. He found out about their language. Some of them sent out the same sounds for each situation, and these were already being studied by students. And—how amazing!—a man was four hundred times taller than an ant and weighed about three millions times as much!

On the next fine day Ladis went out in search of Mufra. He was carrying a tile, painted white, with a single letter P drawn in black for his bird Piccolo's tomb.

'I'd like to see where Piccolo is,' he said to Mufra.

'Right. Shall I make you small?'

'No, I'll take you.'

Mufra gave Ladis the directions and they set off. They soon reached the place they were aiming for. A group of worker ants from Mufra's nest were busy covering the place with a mound of earth. Ladis put a ring of white stones round the grave so that he would recognise it later. He and Mufra worked together, though in fairness it must be said that Mufra sat very comfortably on Ladis's shoulder. They set up the tombstone and Ladis said the Lord's Prayer.

On the way back they talked a bit about what he had read in his books, but very soon Mufra said:

'Aren't you going to ask if anything's happened?'

'What could have happened in such a short time?' Ladis asked, a bit alarmed.

'We've done what you said: we've warned the other nests. And we found that seven of them have already been attacked and occupied by the enemy, and all the ants in them are dead or chased out. We're gathering up as many as we can.'

The end was near, Ladis realised.

'Let me do something about it,' he said. 'My uncle's found some of those Argentine ants in the stable and cowshed. He could put poison down in their nests.'

'And who's going to show him their nests?' said Mufra sharply.

'Me.'

'But you promised . . .'

'All right,' said Ladis, quickly.

'You mustn't interfere, Ladis. Besides, there is still hope. If the weather goes on like this we'll be safe for another year.'

'Why?'

'Haven't you noticed it's getting colder sooner than last year?'

'I've noticed there are more clouds, that it's raining more, and that . . .'

'Well, that's why. In winter, ants rest and don't fight.'

But Ladis knew that next summer the fighting would begin all over again. He had simply got to find a way of fighting the Argentine ants, who had put his friends into such a terrible situation. He was beginning to have an idea, but he kept it to himself.

Suddenly he yelled: 'Hang on tight!'

'Got it, got it!' he cried, as he rose to his feet again. A terrified-looking lizard peeped out from the hollow of his hand.

'Now what, you rascal?' Ladis said excitedly. 'Because if it wasn't you the other day, it must have been your sister, wasn't it?'

'What are you going to do with it, Ladis?' Mufra asked anxiously.

'Whatever you say. You were in the same danger.'

'Let it go, then. It likes living just as much as you and me.'

Ladis hesitated.

'Won't you let me cut off its tail, at least?'

'Certainly not! It may grow again, but it means it's dishonoured before the others.'

Ladis freed the lizard, and it shot away and hid. If it was the one they had seen the other day, it must have had a sharp lesson.

The weather was, in fact, growing colder. Autumn seemed to be coming early, which would suit Mufra and the others. It was then that Ladis decided to put the idea he had thought of into practice: this idea was to get his uncle to block up all the nearby Argentine ants' nests. Mufra had told him not to interfere but she would never know; she was far too busy digging her own nest deeper, to take in fugitives from the other nests.

Together Ladis and his uncle searched for the nests, carefully identifying them with the magnifying glass, and while Ladis told his uncle all kinds of odd things about insect life, they blocked up the mouths of the nests. It took time because, as Ladis knew, ants never have cities with a single door. These condemned ants were very clever, and sealed up their own entrances and exits so perfectly that you could hardly find them.

One afternoon, when Ladis was working alone among the nests, he made a strange discovery: a rare plant that he examined all over and then put into his basket to ask Uncle Floro about.

'Look at this funny plant,' he said, when he got home that evening. 'It's got no roots!'

Uncle Floro picked up the strange object, which was as spiky as a thistle. He examined it all over and then burst out laughing.

'Funny plant, I must say! It's a hedgehog! Come and see.'

And they took the strange animal into the kitchen.

'He must have gone to sleep quite recently,'

said Uncle Floro.

They put him near the fire, still curled up in a ball, and sat down to wait. Ladis looked through his magnifying glass and tried to find the creature's head.

'Don't worry, he'll bring it out himself,' said Uncle Floro.

Soon afterwards the hedgehog began to wake up and a small rat-like head appeared among the spikes. Ladis roared with laughter. Much later the hedgehog tried to get on his feet, and tottered about like a drunkard.

'He looks like a bear,' said Ladis. 'I'm going to call him Nicholas.'

Nicholas filled several afternoons very happily for Ladis. Trickster and the cats wanted to play with their new visitor but he would curl up into a ball and the other animals would prick themselves on his spikes.

It was three or four days since he had seen Mufra when Ladis decided to visit her one afternoon, in particular to tell her about the arrival of Nicholas. He was going towards her nest with his magnifying glass when a grasshopper gripped his shoulder and he heard a stricken voice saying:

'Run Ladis! The attack has started!'

Chapter VIII

The grasshopper shot away with Mufra, leaving Ladis thunderstruck. When he realised what was happening, his first thought was to fetch a weapon—a stone, a stick, anything. Then he realised that no weapon would be any use on such an occasion—that was the ants' strength—and he dashed over in the direction of the nest.

Soon he saw long lines of Argentine ants advancing in the same direction, although separate from one another. As he ran he tried to disorganise and terrify them by stamping on them. But he didn't delude himself. He knew the ants' strong point perfectly well and the way they defended themselves. It isn't easy to kill an insect out-of-doors, especially with a weapon as slow as a foot. Insects can find any number of places to shelter in the uneven ground, among the tiniest stones, in the grass and among the plants. When Ladis attacked them, the ants appeared a little later under the soles of his sandals, alive and kicking.

The lines advanced like the spokes of a wheel towards the centre, destroying everything on their way. In spite of himself Ladis occasionally stopped and turned his magnifying glass on some particular part of the ground: other small creatures—caterpillars, earthworms, glow-worms, ladybirds, woodlice, crickets, grasshoppers and even scorpions— fled from the battlefield, often unsuccessfully, for they were liable to be caught and carved up in a moment. The ants who had captured a prize dropped out of the march and retreated to safeguard their booty.

When Ladis reached Mufra's nest he could see that no fighting was going on there yet. Mufra was organising the battle very intelligently and he could see that she had managed to distract the main part of the advancing column at particular places, presumably to keep it off her small, crowded city. Ladis looked round and saw that the circle was a large one, but complete.

The Argentine ants were approaching their objective from every side. Ladis realised they must have numbers to spare, because other heavy columns were moving away in other directions. Above the main centres of the fighting, dragonflies flew very low. Mufra and her captains were organising defence from the air.

Ladis moved away a little and saw the assailing columns surprised by rapid, unexpected attacks. His heart swelled with delight as he thought: 'Isn't Mufra brave and clever!'

He turned his glass on one of the whirling spots where the fight was hardest. The strength of the Argentine ants lay in their numbers. They did not attack head on, but two or three of them would surround each one of Mufra's

ants and, when they managed to seize it by a
leg, shook it violently against the ground, while
the others leapt on it and in a moment bit off
its legs, leaving it incapable of escape or self-
defence.

By going very close to them, Ladis could see what terrible use both sides made of their jaws. Mufra's ants, who were fatter, sometimes managed to chop small Argentine ants into two. They used their stings and the sticky poison in the form of a pulverised gas that paralysed their enemies and allowed the great warriors to chop off their heads with a single movement of their pincers. A strong, disagreeable smell, like that of a chemist's shop, arose.

Some 'crazy' ants would suddenly appear where the fighting was fiercest, and, feeling confident in their own swiftness, would seize a corpse and vanish with it as fast as they had come. Yet Ladis didn't see many dead.

On several occasions Ladis shouted a warning to Mufra, of dangers only he could see, from his normal size. He realised that although he longed to become small and fight beside his friends as one of them, it would be very little use.

76

The sheer number of Argentine ants carried everything before them. Their tightly packed columns even walked over those who were fighting, then marched on to the nest. Ladis went closer to it. Several dragonflies were wheeling above. The enemy had reached the doors of the nest.

The earth seemed to open up under Ladis's magnifying glass, as the city's small entrances unexpectedly opened wide. Through the cracks poured dozens of mighty warriors, who hurled themselves into the fight, for the nest's false roofs meant it could be emptied at any given moment, much faster than its ordinary peacetime doorways would have allowed.

Ladis knew there were still a great many large warriors inside, their huge heads blocking the entrances to the rooms where the larvae and the main food stores were kept.

His heart was beating violently and he decided to intervene by stamping hard on the

Argentine ants' rearguard. Then a dragonfly landed on his shoulder and he heard Mufra calling excitedly.

'Ladis, you're not to interfere!' she cried. 'I told you about this so that you could come along and learn things known to very few boys, not so that you could stamp on our enemies.'

'But you're crazy,' said Ladis. 'There are millions of them!'

'I'm not crazy. It would be cowardly of you and cowardly of me. Whatever you do we're lost, and I'm going to give the order to retreat. Come near the nest, and don't interfere.'

Ladis obeyed, feeling powerless. He went as close to the nest as he could. On every side stretched the terrible ring of Argentine ants, in a dense mass; then suddenly Mufra's ants managed to clear a way through them and along this path the workers began to appear, carrying the larvae in their mouths. The retreat began and Mufra's warriors were trying to protect it.

The Argentine ants must have realised what
was happening for they respected the strip
along which Mufra's ants were retreating in
good order. But further on, when the battlefield
had changed from the dark colour of the

fighters to the off-white of the larvae and provisions brought up from below, they attacked
again and captured their enemy's children and
provisions—but without hurting them.

It was very odd: Ladis could see that once
their treasure had been taken from them,
Mufra's ants resigned themselves to fleeing
slowly and calmly, without any obvious goal.
They had lost, and that was that. They seemed
to realise it quite well.

The battle lasted nearly five hours and the
sun was beginning to sink behind the distant
hills. Ladis looked round for Mufra. A very few
dragonflies were still flying over the battlefield.
He felt sure that if Mufra pricked him to make
him small he would hear the noise of the
battle, the screams and hisses of the ants and
the clang of their shiny black armour.

'Mufra,' he shouted.

A dragonfly landed gently on his hand.

'It's all over, Ladis. We've been defeated.'

Ladis looked at her in silence, near to tears.

'Have the bad ants won?' he asked.

'They are not "bad ants", Ladis; they're just more numerous and maybe they're better. When they've won everywhere they'll settle down and be more useful than we were.'

Mufra saw that Ladis was ready to cry, and went on: 'We were lost from the start, Ladis. In order to conquer you've got to be able to attack, and we couldn't possibly have expelled the Argentine ants from their territory. This has been one of the greatest battles I've ever seen. But something made them come here. Something quite outside themselves—because they would never have come all at once, if it had been up to them. They're attacking three of our nests at once, and do you know why I think it is? I think they're here because they're fleeing themselves.'

Ladis thought at once of what he and Uncle Floro had done to the Argentine nests, and felt terrible remorse. Mufra had told him not to interfere and he had disobeyed her. And because of him, the attack had begun. But he dared not confess it, thinking that Mufra would never forgive him. How difficult it was to intervene in things you didn't really understand!

'Mufra,' he said. 'I've been thinking a lot, during this fighting. At first I thought I'd build you a nest that could never be attacked. But then ... Come along with me!' he said suddenly. 'You can live in the farm yard till I go to Madrid, and then I'll take you with me in a matchbox. You'll be near me for ever, in a flower-pot of my mother's, and I'll protect you and look after you my whole life.'

Mufra laughed sadly. Then Ladis noticed that her central leg on the right side and her left antenna were both twisted.

'Why, you're wounded!'

'It doesn't matter.'

'Does it hurt very much?'

'Other things hurt more.'

'Will you come?'

'I can't abandon my people.'

Ladis tried to catch the dragonfly that was carrying Mufra, but it leapt aside and landed out of reach.

'Mufra, I promise I won't do anything!'

The dragonfly landed again, this time on his shoulder.

'Ladis, let's be friends for ever. Don't try and capture me. Have you forgotten that I could have made you small, and shut you up in our nest?'

Ladis realised she was right. He looked about him and saw that the Argentine ants were occupying the nest; some of them were cleaning it, and others were following those who had fled, to chase them further away, rather than for any other reason.

'Do you hate them now?'

'No, Ladis. The Argentine ants have done

only what was necessary to occupy the nests. They need a hunting zone that's entirely theirs, just as we do. They have taken it, but only because they need it. If you look, you'll see that there aren't many dead.'

'But what about your children?'

'They will look after them and feed them until they're grown up.'

'And then?'

'Then,' said Mufra, shakily, 'our children will have forgotten us and live in peace with them.'

In a slow, painful procession, Mufra's wounded ants were now moving away.

'You must go home, Ladis. And I must follow my people. We have got to carry on. We'll look for a new shelter. Maybe when the Argentine ants have dominated everything they will let us live in peace. Goodbye, Ladis. I'll remember you as long as I live.'

'And I'll remember you.'

The sun was about to set. The dragonfly took to flight, and followed the defeated column. Ladis went a little nearer and saw Mufra get off her aeroplane and limp across to join a long line of her defeated people. He was so shocked that it never occurred to him to ask if they would meet again. Tears rolled slowly down his cheeks as he waved goodbye.

As his friends moved across towards the lake and Argentine ants were celebrating their victory, Ladis set off for home. A drizzle had begun to fall.

Chapter IX

That night Ladis ate no supper. Uncle Floro and Aunt Lola could not discover why. All he said was:

'I just don't feel like it.'

They offered him fruit and milk.

Finally Aunt Lola took a glass of milk to his room.

When he was left in the dark Ladis realised that he could not sleep, tormented as he was by the thought that he was responsible for everything that had happened, since he had persecuted and poisoned the Argentine ants, stopped up their nests and driven them across to Mufra's territory. If he had done nothing, Mufra and her companions might have been safe for another year.

To console himself, he tried to remember what Mufra had said. He kept remembering that she had said: 'We were lost from the start.' That meant, whether anyone intervened or not. Could Mufra know that he had treated the Argentine ants so badly? Obviously Ladis was guilty of a great deal towards Mufra and her people. Things could not stay as they were and he decided to search for the ants the following day. As he thought this, he fell asleep.

But next day, and the one after that, he couldn't find her, though he searched and searched the lake shore.

'Mufra,' he shouted now and then, and then stopped to give her time to appear.

He saw more Argentine ants than ever. They seemed to dominate everything, in fact to be the only inhabitants of the place.

He had lost his appetite, and Uncle Floro and Aunt Lola were worried. They cooked him special meals and even so they worried when they saw he had to make a great effort to eat at all.

'What's happened to you?' they asked. 'Have you eaten anything bad while you were out?'

They took his temperature, and he had no fever. One day they put him to bed. And that same day, in the afternoon, the telegram came. Uncle Floro merely told him that his mother was ill and he must go home. Ladis was frightened, and then they handed him the telegram to read.

'Petra ill. Need Ladis's help. Nothing serious. Love Feliciano.'

It was quite near the end of summer, but Ladis burst into tears. Uncle Floro and Aunt Lola thought it was because his mother was ill and he had to go back to town. But Ladis's sorrow had another reason: Mufra. How could he go without talking to her just once more?

When he least knew what to do or what to think, that same night, he found Mufra on his pillow.

'Ladis, I've come to ask for your help.'

Ladis took her in his hand and kissed her.

'I've searched for you so often,' he said.

'Look, Ladis, after we left you we walked for days, exploring the countryside in search of shelter. We had almost decided on one, when suddenly the Argentine ants landed on us again. They weren't the same ones, but those who had gone to invade the other three nests—the ones I told you about. They had conquered them and were terribly excited. They surrounded us and attacked us.'

Here Mufra had to pause.

'There were few of us, and we were beaten, wounded, without our children and with no food except what we had managed to get on the march. We stood up to them, but this time they crushed us. Only five of us were left.'

'Where are the others?'

'Very near here, waiting until I've talked to

you. You offered to take me to Madrid. Could you do it now, and take the five of us that are left?'

'Of course I could!' said Ladis, radiant.

'We only ask you for shelter during the winter.'

Ladis was delighted. He told Mufra that he had had a telegram and was to leave for Madrid next day.

'Besides,' he said, 'my book gives very clear instructions on building artificial ants' nests.'

'Artificial moonshine, Ladis. You told me your mother had a flower-pot.'

'Yes, a good big one.'

'Right. Well, the only thing you need do is put it indoors, because I know it's very cold in Madrid.'

'So we will, then. And besides, I'll keep you warm with straw or whatever you say. And I'll bring you food every day. And . . .'

'Later, when it's spring,' Mufra interrupted,

'we'll have new ants. Three of my four companions are female, and they will soon be having children. The fourth's a male, and badly
wounded.'

'I'll get a big matchbox,' said Ladis, 'the
kind that takes those long wooden matches
Uncle Floro uses to light his pipe.'

They agreed on everything and parted. Ladis
had plenty to do, packing up. He was taking
Nicholas, the hedgehog, as well, but would
leave him asleep in the yard throughout the
winter, wrapped in rags. Mufra had told him
that in spring he could let him loose in the right
sort of place, outside the city or in a garden or
a park.

Next day Quique arrived with his van and
Ladis said goodbye to his uncle and aunt and all
their animals. Then they set off, with Aunt
Lola shouting after them:

'Write straight away and tell us how your
mother is!'

Ladis made a gesture, which meant he promised he would. He was worried about his mother, who had been ill last winter. But his more immediate worry was to stop the matchbox, which was in the top pocket of his shirt, jumping out when the van bumped on the road. In it, with a little earth moistened with sugared water, as Mufra had told him, were Mufra and her four companions.

This second summer, his departure was very dull. No insects in their thousands came along to say goodbye, as they had done last time. But Ladis was happy because he was taking Mufra with him.

On the bus, he found himself sitting next to a fat, kind, chatty woman who kept bothering him with questions and stopped him talking to Mufra. At last she noticed that he was carrying a matchbox in his hand, and occasionally raising it to his ear.

'What have you got in that, dear?' she asked.

'A cricket,' said Ladis quickly.
'Doesn't he sing?'

'No, he's constipated.'

Ladis opened the box slightly and put it close to his ear. And at once he heard Mufra's voice saying the one word:

'Liar!'